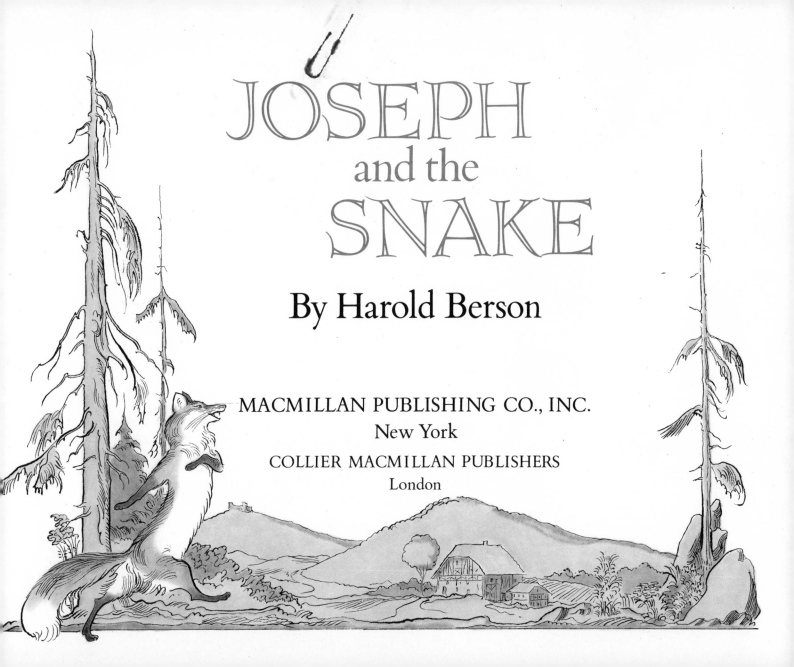

JOSEPH
and the
SNAKE

By Harold Berson

MACMILLAN PUBLISHING CO., INC.
New York
COLLIER MACMILLAN PUBLISHERS
London

Macmillan Publishing Co., Inc.
866 Third Avenue, New York, N.Y. 10022
Collier Macmillan Canada, Ltd.
Printed in the United States of America
Typographic Design by Ben Birnbaum

10   9   8   7   6   5   4   3   2   1

LIBRARY OF CONGRESS CATALOGING IN PUBLICATION DATA
Berson, Harold.   Joseph and the snake.
SUMMARY: Only a fox's cleverness saves Joseph
from being eaten by the hungry and ungrateful snake
whose life he saved.
[1. Foxes—Fiction.   2. Snakes—Fiction]   I. Title.
PZ7.B4623Jo   [E]   78-12317   ISBN 0-02-709200-3

JOSEPH and the SNAKE

Once there was a boy named Joseph. He was the servant of a prince who made him work very hard for very little money. One day Joseph put an apple and a crust of bread in his pocket and set off to seek his fortune.

After a while, he saw a large snake stuck under a heavy stone.

"Please," cried the snake, "help me out of here before I die of hunger."

Joseph felt sorry for him and, taking a heavy stick, he lifted the stone enough to free the snake.

The snake reared up. "I'm sorry, but I am fainting from hunger. I'll have to eat the nearest thing around—you!"

"After what I did for you?" said Joseph, offering the snake his apple and bread crust instead.

"That just won't be enough," said the snake. "Look how long and thin I am."

"Please don't eat me," cried Joseph. "It's not fair to eat the person who helped you."

"Well," said the snake, "why don't we ask the first three strangers we meet on the road if it is fair or not? If they all think that I should eat you, then I shall."

So Joseph agreed because he had no choice.

Soon they met a dog.

"Oh handsome dog," said Joseph, "we need your advice. This snake would have died if I had not helped him out from underneath a heavy stone. Now he wants to eat me. Is that fair?"

The dog growled crossly. "Nothing and no one is fair. My master kicked me out because I chased a chicken around the barnyard. Your problems don't concern me." The dog shuffled off in a cloud of dust.

Joseph and the snake walked on a little farther and met a very tired-looking horse.

"I saved this snake's life and now he wants to eat me. Is that fair?" Joseph asked.

"What is fair?" snorted the horse. "When I was strong and healthy, I pulled the carriage of a lord. Now that I am weak and sick, I've been tossed out. Your problems are of no concern to me." The horse walked wearily away.

Joseph and the snake walked on and met a cunning fox.

"I saved this snake from certain death when he was stuck under a stone," said Joseph. "Now he wants to eat me. Is that fair?"

"In order to answer that question, I must see exactly what happened," said the fox.

"We will show you just how it was," said Joseph, and all three walked back to the rock.

Joseph moved the stone and the snake slid under it. Then Joseph let the stone fall back in place so that the snake was stuck again.

"Is that the way you were when Joseph took the stone off your back?" the fox asked the snake.

"Yes," answered the snake. "I can't budge."

"Well, stay there then," said the fox.

So Joseph was saved from being eaten.

"Thank you, thank you, dear and kind fox. What can I do to repay you?" he asked.

"Well," answered the fox, "give *me* something to eat. I'm so hungry I could eat for a week."

"Follow me then," said Joseph. "I'll help you get into the Prince's storehouse, where there is more than enough food for you."

Joseph led the fox to the Prince's storehouse and helped him climb in. The fox was eating frantically when the door burst open.

"Ah," cried the Prince, clutching Joseph by the collar, "I saw it all."

The poor hungry fox jumped out of the window and was gone.

"Spare me," cried Joseph. "I will show you a treasure beyond your wildest dreams. It is buried beneath a stone not far from here."

"It had better be a large and sparkling treasure or you will pay dearly," said the Prince with a scowl.

Joseph led the Prince to the stone that was pinning down the snake. "The treasure is underneath," he said.

The Prince paid no attention to the seemingly lifeless snake as he raised the stone.

Out leaped the snake, who by that time was extremely hungry. He swallowed the Prince without so much as saying a word.

Joseph moved into the Prince's house and lived happily ever after. The fox could always count on an excellent meal whenever he passed that way, which he did very often.

Harold Berson was born and raised in Los Angeles. He graduated from the University of California at Los Angeles with a degree in sociology and worked for a time in the Bureau of Public Assistance before deciding to become an illustrator. After studying in Paris on the G.I. Bill, he received his first commission in 1958, and since that time has illustrated over eighty books, some of which he has written himself. Among the children's books he has illustrated are Dorothy O. Van Woerkom's tales of the Middle East, Abu Ali *and* The Friends of Abu Ali.

Mr. Berson and his wife, Paula, who is also an artist, make their home in New York City but travel in Europe and the Middle East whenever they can.